TALONS OF POWER

GETTING LOST

MRIDINI MISHRA

Made with ♥ on the Notion Press Platform
www.notionpress.com

I WOULD LIKE TO DEDICATE THIS STORY TO ALL
THOSE BOOKWORMS AND DELULU PEOPLE

----*---WHO LOVE TO READ----*-----

Contents

Foreword   *xi*

Prologue   *xiii*

PART 1

1. Chapter 1   3
2. Chapter 2   5
3. Chapter 3   7
4. Chapter 4   10
5. Chapter 5   13
6. Chapter 6   15
7. Chapter 7   18
8. Chapter 8   21
9. Chapter 9   23
10. Chapter 10   27
11. Chapter 11   29
12. Chapter 12   31
13. Chapter 13   34
14. Chapter 14   37
15. Chapter 15   39
16. Chapter 16   42
17. Chapter 17   45
18. Chapter 18   48
19. Chapter 19   51
20. Chapter 20   54
21. Chapter 21   56

Contents

22. Chapter 22   58

23. Chapter 23   61

24. Chapter 24   64

25. Chapter 25   66

26. Chapter 26   68

27. Chapter 27   70

28. Chapter 28   73

29. Chapter 29   76

30. Chapter 30   78

31. Chapter 31   82

32. Chapter 32   84

33. Chapter 33   87

FOREWORD

PROLOGUE

HAYAMI YAMAGUCHI-

The main character of this story is Hayami. She's a very adventurous girl who love a lot many silly things to do. She finds happiness in every small things. Even the tiniest ones. Unfortunatly, she was an orphan. Her parents left her when she was of five. They had erased all her memory before living her in an orphanage.

NOW EVERYTHING IS A MYSTERY AND SURPRISE~

You'll soon get to know about what's in there. Go on and explore...

DIAMOND COMMUNITY- Queen Splendour

*This is the highest and the richest community.

*They are usually occupated in buisness and trading.

*It is situated at the south-east of the PHILIA

SNOW COMMUNITY- Queen Avalanche

*It's all covered with snow and Sun comes out there only once in a month.

*They are known the best suppliers for electronic items.

*It's situated at the North or Top of PHILIA

RAINBIRDS COMMUNITY- QUEEN NATURE

*They are usually covered with trees and have very dense forests.

*They are known the best suppliers for the fruits and vegetables

*It's situated at the South of PHILIA

CLOUD WORLD COMMUNITY- Queen Thunderstorm

*It's situated on the North-east of PHILIA.

*People from there, usually work for army to protect the whole PHILIA.

*It's very foggy there.

MAIN CHARACTERS OF THIS STORY-

HAYAMI YAMAGUCHI- Hayami means Rare beauty

YUKI HAYASHI (Hayami's friend)- Yuki means Snow

AKUMA KASHIWAGI (Hayami's friend)- Akuma means Demon ore Devil

OSPREY KASHIWAGI (Akuma's brother)- Osprey is a bird

AKARI OGAWA (Hayami's friend)- Akari means Bright Village

HANA YAMASHITA (Hayami's friend)- Hana means flower

TOSHIRO YAMAMOTO (Hayami's friend)- Toshiro means Talented

HIROSHI YAMAGUCHI (Hayami's father)- Hiroshi means prosperous

SAYURI YAMAGUCHI (Hayami's mother)- Sayuri means Lily

AKARI YAMAGUCHI (Hayami's elder sister)- Akari means Beloved Child

HINATA YAMAGUCHI (Hayami's younger sister)- Hinata means Sunny place or Sunflower

YURIE NAKAMURA (Hayami's teacher)- Yurie means Ghost

MURIEL (Hayami's pet macaw)- Muriel means Bright sea

LATE. QUEEN SUNSHINE- The old Queen of the Diamond community

QUEEN SPLENDOUR- The recent Queen of the Diamond community

QUEEN YASHA- The recent Queen of the Nightpowers

PART 1

---------*--------Meet HAYAMI-----------*---------

I
Chapter 1

Hayami didn't think that she was the right person for a great and 'Big Heroic Destiny', but she had always dreamt that.

Oh, she wanted to be. She wanted to be the great saviour and ruler of a magical world, glorious, pretty and brave. She always wanted to do all the beautiful and wonderful things expected from her, very passionatly. She wanted to observe the world, figure out what was wrong and broken, and then-fix it. She just wanted the whole world full of serenity.

But sadly, she wasn't a natural born herione, which she always wanted to become. She had almost no legendary qualities at all! She was just like other people was had just 'I'M STILL ALIVE' as a nice quality. She was okay in studies and in fighting but that 'okay-okay' was not going to help her to change the world.

"Hayami! Your turn is next for the obstacle run, go and wear your band fast!" Shouted Yurie as she broke into Hayami's reverie. Yurie was Hayami's teacher and as her name itsef says that, Yurie means GHOST, she acted like one. She was way to scary and terrfingly dangerous to be a teacher of. Hayami got onto the track. "Hayami take your position!" Said the coach. "All the best Hayami!" Shouted Akari, her father's friend's daughter, basically her friend. Hayami smiled at her.

And the time starts... NOW!"

Hayami ran as fast as she could. The sun was shining bright in the sky as Hayami got tired in the half of the track. She could hear the students chattering outside the tracks. "Feint to the LEFT! Roll RIGHT! Jump properly! Run FAST!" Yurie yelled. Even though she was scary yet, she cared about Hayami a lot. She knew that Hayami has some will powers or abilities, she can achieve something small. Or even bigger.

Hayami ducked down to the left, jumped upon a stool, not the small one a, a large one, but ofcourse, rolled the wrong way. "WHICH LEFT WAS THAT USELESS?" Yurie shouted hard. As Hayami took the wrong roll, off she went out of the track adn leading to her hurting and stabbed toe. "Oww!" She groaned in pain. Akari and Hana rushed to her for help. "Useless creature", Yurie whispered underneath her breath. "Maam even though she rolled the wrong way, she has taken the least time to complete the race. Rolling made it easier for her to reach the finish line", said the coach. Yurie looked at Hayami in disgust. "She has won ma'am".

"Well done Hayami!" Akari exclaimed as Hayami got the trophy handed over by the principle. "Thanks!" Hayami said happily.

II
Chapter 2

Hayami.

Hayami Yamaguchi was an eight- year old child who was adopted by Mr. Hiroshi Yamaguchi and Mrs. Sayuri Yamaguchi, when she was of five. She had very pretty blue-coloured eyes along with hairs. She was very fair. Her nickname was Kiyomi. She loved being call this from everyone.

Mr. Yamaguchi belonged to the 'DIAMOND Community' which was the highest one. He had a very rich company of Golds and Diamonds. Well, it was so big that, it was worth being call and empire. 'THE YAMAGUCHI EMPIRE'.

The second eldest, Mrs. Yamaguchi was no other than her husband's accountant. Although, she didn't work much in her company but waste her time in listening to other assisstant's talks. She should have been called a 'nosy neighbour'. She hated Hayami. That was because, when they adopted her, they didn't know of which community she was. She didn't want to adopt her at the first sight but, her father, he fell in love with her beautiness thus, named her Hayami, which means 'RARE BEAUTY'.

Now, here comes her elder sister, Aiko Yamaguchi. Who wasn't a psycho but sometimes acted like one. As her name itself says Aiko, or 'BELOVED CHILD', she was loved by all. Specially by her mother. She was a kind of tomboy.

Hinata Yamaguchi, Hayami's little sister was of just three-years old. She was very cute and loved Hayami a lot. She loved writing stories and reading them.

So this family of five people, is a very rich and prosperous family in the whole world. According to the people. They always lived happily and treated everyone with love and care. But this story's main character is only one,-

HAYAMI YAMAGUCHI...

III
Chapter 3

Mr. and Mrs. Yamaguchi were chilling with their children on a dark winter's day, when the yellow fog hung so thick and heavy in the streets of PHILIA that the lamps were lighted and the stop windows blazed with gas as they do at night. A beautiful and petite little girl sat on her father's lap with a queer old-fashioned thoughtfulness in her lovely eyes.

"Dad, I'm hungry" said Hayami in a low little voice which was almost a whisper. "Oh, hi hungry! I'm Dad". Dad I'm not joking, I'm seriously starving!"She said. "I know that you're not joking but wait are you seriously starving? Starving Yamaguchi?" he said in a giggly way. Aiko was staring at her father in disgust. "Dad", Hayami said in a cold tone as if she would eat him only. "Okay my child, let's go to a nearby cafe! We-" "No need!" shouted Sayuri interrupting Hiroshi's idea. "Mom! please, I'm hungry too!" said Aiko. "Okay if you say so dear" a sudden change in her voice happened from devil to angel. As they walked they reached a cafe named,"Nakamura Cafe". It was a quite place with dim yellow lights but looked really royal. They found a place to sit and Hinata quickly grabbed the menu card just to play something-something.

Sayuri and Hiroshi orderd Dora cakes with juice whereas, Aiko ordered Pizza. Hinata ordered Kimchi and Hayami ordered one bowl veg ramen. At the end Sayuri thought of ordering a scoop of strawberry ice cream for all. "Waiter! Can we have one scoop of strawberry ice-cream each?" sked Sayuri in a polite but rude manner. "No!" shouted Hiroshi and Hinata at the same time. "I mean t-that we all can have b-but except Hayami", said Hiroshi. Hayami felt really bad. His father and little sister never allowed her to eat anything realated to strawberry. 'God Knows Why'. "But dad,why don't you ever let Hayami eat strawberry or anything amde up with it?" asked Aiko being a little happy as she thought she'll get Hayami's part of ice-cream too. "Just" said Hinata.

"Are you Aiko's dad Hinata?" said Sayuri teasingly but she also wanted to know why. "Yah, Just" said Hiroshi too. Hayami was taught to stay away from starwberries as far as she can. "Dad, can I have vanilla instead?" Hiroshi nodded and Aiko frowned. As they completed their meal, they walked to their home. They had planned to have a family sleepover. However, Sayuri and Aiko rejected that offer and they went to their own room. As soon as Hinata lied on the bed, she slept, Hayami lied in the middle of her father and sister. It was very cold outside. "Dad", she said in a curious low voice. "Why do you never let me eat strawberries?" Hiroshi said in a low husky voice. "You are too young to understand." "Then why does Hinata know about it?" Hayami questioned. "Hinata doesn't know, she just heared me saying no to you while eating strawberries so she started copying me."

"Oooo, fascinating! Am I allergic to it or something?"
She asked. "You'll soon get to know Kiyomi! Now sleep.
Goodnight!!!" He said. "Goodnight Dad" she said when she
still wanted to talk more.

IV
Chapter 4

Nearby ten years had passed since the Yamaguchi's had woken up to find their new daughter in an orphanage, but their city, hasn't changed at all. The Sun rose on the same tidy front gardens and lit up the little yet, various flowers."Morning Dad!" said Hayami while yawing and rubbing her eyes. "Morning my child! You woke so early? It's just 6!" Said Hiroshi in a happy tone. " Ya, I had a nice sleep. Morning Mom!" She said while giving a pause. "Morning", said Sayuri in a bit kind manner. As the years had passed, Sayuri's rudeness towards Hayami was getting lesser, But! Not gone. "Is Aiko still asleep ?" Sayuri asked in a concertive manner. "Umm, Yeah" She said thinking Sayuri will get mad at her.

Hayami got freshed and went to the dining area for the breakfast. Hinata was awake too. Everybody settleddown and started to eat after mumbling a short prayer. "Morning pops!" Aiko said in a sleepy way. "Do you even know what's the time right now?" Hiroshi said in a loud but worried manner. It was 10:31 AM. "Don't shout at her!" Said Sayuri glaring at Mr. Yamaguchi. Aiko sat down on one of the chair. "Pookie, you should brush your teeth first!" said Hinata in a low cute voice. "Shut up!" Shouted Aiko. "Behave Aiko!" Exclaimed Hayami as she finished her food. Aiko was giving a cold look to her.

"Can you pleaes turn on the TV for your pops Aiko?" He said while pouting with food in his mouth. "No !" said Aiko. "No problem, We can't even except this from you" Hayami gave her a disgusting look while she turned the TV on, and handed the remote to Mr. Yamaguchi. "12 people went missing in some districts of Tokyo. The last place they were seen was near a forest. Probably a Tropical rainforest. Some of our agents have seen a bracelet of black colour made up of black pure diamond. We are tr-"

"Oh my gosh!" shiuted Aiko in between of the news report. "I got to know that three of them were my followrs, Mom!" she tried fake crying. "Oh Aiko it's okay, there just three of your followers, think that what have been their families gone through."

"But my situation is much sadder mom!" "It has been known that there is going to be a lot of fight and a new community is going to be formed. What will be it's name, no one know till now. But if you subscribe our channel we'll ensure th-" "Here they go again" said Hinata while she left out a deep breath. Hayami was listening to it very closely with curiousity filled in her eyes. She slowly went to her bedroom and took out some scrolls to search something.

"I want to know more about that" she whispered to herself in a low husley voice. After finding a lot, finally she wrote some information on a scroll.

"12 people went missing in the region of Rain Birds community and the last places they were seen was near a tropical rainforest. This same situation had happened approximately two yers ago. Ten people went missing and one was found till now. Oooo fascinating!" Hayami blinked at herself in mirror. " I can't go out of my community untill I completed my studies. But I want to!"

V
Chapter 5

"Sista! What are you thinking?" Aiko came to her room while listening to some music on her headphones and eating an apple. "I'll tell you but promise you won't tell it to anybody". Hayami said quietly. "What?" Aiko said confused. "First TAKE OFF YOUR HEADPHONES!" Hayami exclaimed. "Oh sorry!" She took off her headphones and sat down beside her. "Apple?" asked Aiko. "Umm, no, I'm not that famished", said Hayami. "An apple a day keeps the doctor away! No problem if you don't want to eat. I'm really scared of injections". Aiko said. "True. AN APPLE A DAY KEEPS THE DOCTOR AWAY- IF YOU THROW IT HARD ENOUGH ON HIS HEAD..." Hayami said. The both started laughing. "Okay now listen, don't you think that the queen of our community is doing very unfair with us?" I mean that, why can't children walk out of our community untill we finish our studies?" Remarked Hayami. "Umm, ya you've got the point but, we can't even step out!" Akari said. "But I want to!" Hayami bemoaned. "It's a terrible idea, I'm telling you". Aiko said. "Guys what about the mountain hole?" Hinata said that in a rush, jumping into the brief pause in the conversation. "Unless your name is google, stop acting like you know everything", Aiko said. Hayami giggled. "Mountain hole? What's that?" Hayami asked. "Mountain hole is one more place from where we can try to sneak out of here". "So let's escape!" Hayami said. "Oh Hayami, don't be ridiculous" Aiko said. "It's way to small", Hinata explained. "But Hinata you can go! You are very small and slim", said Hayami as a light of hope came in her eyes. "It won't work", Hinata said.

"I'm sorry Hayami but, I've gone up to the hole when no one was around", commented Aiko. "Me too", said Hinata. Hayami felt low and slow. She sat down near the mountain hole often enough, watching the cows grazing and nature outside their community, but she'd never gone near it or tried to climb out. Apparently, her own sisters have thought to escape a lot more than she had. "The hole is smaller than you think, I can bearly fit through it. There's no way out," said Aiko said. "But there must be!" Hayami said desperatly. "But what's the matter sistie, why do you wanna go out?" Hinata asked in a cute, almost-a-whisper voice. "I want to find my real parents, I just want to meet them once and ask them that what did I lack in myself," Hayami said with tears in her eyes. "Guess you are right, we'll think about it. But! Promise that no one will tell anything to anyone. Not even to mom and pops", said Aiko. "Promise!" Hinata said. "Promise", Hayami said quietly. The promise was everything for her.

VI
Chapter 6

Hayami had never really believed the legends about her new classmates. Basically, one was a girl and one was a boy. She heard that the community from which she belonged to was... UNKNOWN. Hayami was very excited as she turned off the lights and went to her bed to sleep. She kept thinking-

"*What will I ask them?*" She thought. "*Ahem-Ahem, Hi! I'm Hayami, Hayami Yamaguchi*" She said clearing her throat. "No... That's a bit too formal", she commented. "Hey there! Do you wanna be my friend?" She said staring at herself in the mirror. "And thats's a bit too INFORMAL! Leave it, I'll see it tomorrow." Next Day-

"It's not true, they wouldn't!" Hayami said. "They can! Sometimes the teachers find the new students more attractive. You might have to get down from the post of her favorite student", said Sayori while making one pony of her daughter's while admiring the new comb she bought. "Bye!" Hiroshi said as Hayami climbed the bus and luckily got the first seat. "Bye Dad!, Bye Mom!"

The bus pulled away and stopped at the next stop which it had never before. It was very cold outside almost like Subzero. The door opened and a boy and a girl entered. Surprisingly, they were only Hayami's new classmates or you can say, COMPETITORS.

"Wow! look at your hairs, they seem so magical!" the girl said as she stumbled while climbing the stairs. "Uh, thank you. By the way umm, what's your na-" "Myself Yuki. Yuki Hayashi. You?" "I'm Hayami Yamaguchi". Hayami said as she offered her half of the seat. "Oh, may I sit with you?" Yuki said in an energetic voice. "Ya sure!" Hayami found that girl a bit too extrovert. A macaw came and sat on the bus's window, while gripping it's wings. "Is it yours?" Yuki asked. "No, it's not mine but, it always comes to me, I don't know why. But this macaw is actually very cute", Hayami said lostly. "Maybe, he also likes your hairs!" Yuki said. "Hey! Is that boy also with you?" asked Hayami while giving him a bombastic side eye.

"No. His home is beside mine. He's my neighbour. His family has shifted just a week ago". Yuki said in a disgust manner."I don't know why but he always stays so quiet-quiet. I think he is voiceless, he can't speak"."Ooo fascinating" Hayami said as she thought about the word, VOICELESS. "What's his name?" "I don't know, you only ask him na!" Yuki said if she doesn't want to talk to anyone except that good- looking girl with magical blue hairs. "Hi, What's your name?" She asked as she turned back. "I can't tell you that," he said in a deep cold voice while narrowing his eyes. "I can't tell you that too, it's my community business". "I didin't know that some communities have some secret- keeeoing business too. "Hayami shrugged. The boy started laughing. Yuki looked at Hayami in a **WHAT THE HELL** is this manner.

"Nobody talks to us like that! Where's your sense of awe? Your terror of our power?"he looked at Yuki then at Hayami, but his eyes were teasing. "Us, means your community? And powers? I didn't hear about any community with that much power to get scared of." Hayami said thinking about why he said 'terror of their powers'. Their school was about to come. "Which community do you belong?" Asked Yuki as she was playing with Hayami's fringes. "I don't know". "Me either!" Yuki said surprisingly "I want to tell you something Yuki,I don't know whether you would like to be my friend after that or not," Hayami said fumbling. "Ya sure te-" "What's your name?" The boy interuppted. Hayami thought that she shouldn't tell about it to Yuki right now. It's not the right time. "I'm Yuki!" Yuki said cheerfully. *He tilted his head looking amused,* "I didn't ask you! I asked the girl beside you," he grinned. Hayami glared at him. "Sorry, I can't tell you that. MY COMMUNITY BUISNESS!" She said dramaticlly. "Who knew that sarcasm can grow in a place this cold", he said with a smile. "Will you yell me your name if I tell you mine?" "Nope!" Said Yuki. The boy looked at her looking irritated. "Frankly, I'm not that interested", Hayami turned back and gave him an evil smile. "Okay then, I'll tell you mine anyway", he said while he ruffled his hairs. "If you'll come to see me again, will you?" "Maybe", Hayami called back. "I'm pretty busy'.

"My name", he called. Yuki looked inocently. Hayami pretended like she wasn't listening but, she was. "My name is Akuma Kashiwagi". *"Pretty scary and fierce name he has",* Hayami thought. "Okay, nice. So students today, your first two periods are of games. So you all can go to the ground and umm-ENJOY!" The teacher said. "Yaaaaaaaaaaay!" all the children shouted. Hayami, Akari, Yuki, Hana, and Toshiro went to the ground together.

VII
Chapter 7

Akuma Kashiwagi From a community you should be scared of. A community with very terrible powers. Hayami's head was going round and round as she entered the school premises. "His name is so weird right?" Yuki said. "Ya, I've also never heard of that kind of name anywhere. Not even in any scrolls", said Hayami. "What does it even mean?" Asked Yuki. "We'll see that later. Let's go or you'll be late for your first lecture!" Hayami laughed and Yuki smiled.

As they reached their classroom they saw that Akuma arrived before them. Hayani ignored and Yuki made a disgust face. They both sat infront of Akuma at the first bench. "Hi Hayami!" Hana and Akari came runningband sliding through the granite floor. "Who's this?" Hana remarked looking confused. "Hi, I'm Yuki Hayashi".She said while looking at Hayami's friends. "Hi! Nice to meet you!" said Akari, "By the way Hayami, I thought that I'll sit with you today but umm, It's okay" Akari frowned. "Uhh, If you want then you can sit" Yuki said quietly looking a bit sad. "No Yuki it's alright! Akari it's her first day so I wanted to sit with her to make her feel a bit comfortable. But I promise I'll sit with you tomorrow". Hayami tried to not to mess up anything. "Okay, so then for today, me and Hana willsit together !" Akari hugged Hana happily as Hana tried to jump back before they could touch.

"Goooooooood Moooorrrnnniinngg Maaaaaaaaaaam!" All the children sang together in a chorus. The backbenchers started to laugh. Almost the whole class started to laugh. Yuki was laughing so hard, as if she would pass out. All the children stood up except, *Akuma.* Well, the teacher didn't notice him. He was sitting on the bench with full attitude. Hayami and Yuki glared at him. "Good morning children, please sit down", replied the teacher. "Thaaaaaaaannk Yoooooooou Maaaaaaaaaam!" The children laughed again. Akuma giggled. "Okay so students, we have two new children in our class. Yuki Hayashi and-" "Akuma Kashiwagi", said Akuma as he chiped in the teacher's sentence. "Ya, so please you both come forward and introduce yourselves". Yuki came forward shyly and tucked her hair behind her ears and said, "Goodmorning everyone, I'm Yuki Kashiwagi, and I am 10 years old. I am an extovert and I love making friends. My best friend is, Hayami and I love her hairs, *thank you!*" She want back to her place. "Akuma! Please come forward", the teacher said sweetly. "Hello, I'm Akuma Kashiwagi and I'm 11 years old. I'm an introvert and I love only one thing, TO BE PERSONAL. I hope you all can understand. Thanks!" He let out a sigh and then sat down. "Yuki, Akuma, what are the meaning of your names?" Asked the teacher. "Mine means snow, and I also love winter season", said Yuki. "Mine means devil", Akuma said in a deep voice. "Okay, nice. So students your first two periods are of games. So you all can go to the ground and umm-ENOJOY!" The teacher said. "Yaaaaaaaaay!" All the children shouted. Hayami, Akari, Yuki, Hana adn Toshiro held each others hand. Off they went to the ground.

VIII
Chapter 8

Yuki stared at the ground which was very vast. "Wow! Atleast a thousand cows can fit in this. No wait! maybe a lakh. Hayami laughed at her reaction. "So,as we have two games period consecutively, we should play a game that can last long. Any ideas guys?" said Akari. Hayami felt Akari is always like her sister Aiko. A little bossy, a little trendy and stylish but she was not at all ill-mannered like Aiko. "Guy?!" Aiko said again. No reply. She let out a sigh and then suddenly Akuma came. "Can I join you'all guys if you don't mind?" Yuki and Hayami narrowed their eyes at him. "Ya ofcourse! But only if you can give us an idea what to play", said Hana. "Umm okay, guess we can play mafia?" he said in a manner as if he was thinking that they would say no. "Ya! I vote yes!" shouted Hayami and Akira. They both looked at each other and laughed. "I have never played this game before", said Yuki. "Me too!" said Toshiro. "And I don't like that game", said Hana.

"So we can play 'recreate the history ' game! That's wonderful according to me. All we have to do is to pick any one event happened in history which was very adventurous and then we have to act it out!" exclaimed Akuma. "Ah! I've never played this before but it seems nice!" Remarked Hayami. "Us too! Guess we should play",said evryone. "Okay so let's take the event of the death of our past queen. The queen splendour!" said Toshiro royally. "Have you gone crazy? Queen Splendour is alive, she's our recent queen!" Shouted Yuki. "Oh yeah sorry, so ahem-ahem, once again, let's take the event of the DEATH of our PAST QUEEN. The queen Sunshine!" "Yay!"shouted everyone when Akuma just smiled Hana said-"Okay so,

Yuki will be the queen Sunshine.

Toshiro and I will be the thieves.

Hayami and Akuma will be the prince and princess. The daughter and son of Queen Sunshine.

And Akari will be the director.

IX
Chapter 9

"LIGHTS, CAMERA, AND DISTRACTION"

Yuki : "Okay so here I go, la la la la , I'm the Queen Sunshine of the Diamond community. I'm evryone's sunshine! I'm so very important, rich and, uh- royal- and uh, stuff".

Hayami sighed. Toshiro and Hana hid their smiles while they were behind the bushes.

Yuki : "I'm very rich with a lots of uh,um".

"Treasure! say treasure!" Akari whispered pointing at a pile of Badminton cocks.

Yuki : "Okay so, um, ya! I'm very rich with a lots of treasure. I've been the Queen for ages and ages!"

Yuki went on and on. She laid on the grass dramaticly.

Yuki : "No one dares challenge me for my throne! I'm the strongest Queen who ever lived!"

(She stood up and strutted across the floor). "It's probably because of all my treasure!" *She swept all the badminton cocks towards her and gathered them between her hands.*

Toshiro and Hana: "Did someone said the name of treasure ?" *They bellowed as they leaped out from behind the goal post. Yuki yelped with fright. Yuki : Ahhhh!*

"No ! You're not scared!" Akari called. "You're the big, great and cruel Queen of the Diamonds. Yuki!" *Akari was very strict that time.*

Yuki : "R-right, Rargh! What are these tiny timid thieves doing in my kingdom? I'm no-not at all afraid. I-I shall go out near there and then bite their neck off and stuff them in a volcano!"

Hayami and Akuma were giggling so hard that they had to lie down and cover their faces. Even Akari was making faces like she way trying not to laugh. Hana and Toshiro started circling around Yuki.

Hana : Give us all your treasure! And your children. Toshiro : Or else we have our own ways to take them.

Yuki: I'll not let you take it ! My children are my world. *Yuki stamped her foot as she gave a funny death glare.*

Hana and Toshiro : "Aaaarghh!" *They shouted lunging forward. They all started thrusting and jabbing eachh other. "Don't actually hurt me" Said Yuki getting nervously. "Ofcourse they won't" said Akari. "We're just acting"*

Yuki : "You are not thieves! You all are assassins! You all want to kill me. Aaaaaaaa!!!"

Akuma coughed as soon as they said 'assassin'. His look changed to cold one again from the happy one.

Hana and Toshiro : "Shut up you magnificant Queen! Yaaaaah!!!"

But in the end Queen Sunshine had to die- that was how the history was. Hana and Toshiro stabbled their fake sword in her stomach, shoved on her legs and then at last Hana thrusted the fake knife between her neck as if it went exactly through her heart.

Yuki : "Aaaaaaaaargh" *She howled* "It can't be! I can't die! my kingdom! It will fall apart! My children! They can't live hell in my as beautiful as heaven place. Oh my my. I love you all !!!"

And she collapsed. "Our turn!" said Hayami and Akuma. Hana and Toshiro went towards the directorand Yuki remained there only played dead.

Hayami : Oh no! Our mother! The QUEEN OF THE DIAMONDS IS... **DEAD!** What should we do now? Akuma: Probably leave her here to die?

"No! You have to say 'O my! Guess we have to find a new Queen!" Said Akari.

Akuma: "Oh my my! Guess we have to find a new Queen! Mom!!! You can't leave us!

He started fake crying.

Hayami : "Well now, I think that I should be the Queen. As I'm the youngest, I'll have the longest reign".

Akuma : Why can't there be a King! I'll be the good ruler of our kingdom.

Hana : That we'll decide! Hana and Toshiro creeped out again.

Toshiro : We've got the treasure. Now we're hungry! They both roared.

Hana : We get to pick right? So we'll eat this boy,- 'Sunny'

Hayami : No! You can't kill my brother!

Toshiro : So, we'll kill you then! Splendour!

Akuma : Don't kill her I'm ready to die! Then Toshiro started to com near him.

"Wow Nice Game!" Said Yuki. "Stop talking!" Hayami said poking her with one finger. "You're dead".

And then Toshiro stabbled him on his stomach. Akuma : Aaaaaargh!!! He howled in fake pain.

Hayami : "No! You can't die! Guess I have to be the queen now."

Everyone together : Thank you! The story of Our recent Queen 'Splendour' is over. Thank you.

X
Chapter 10

They all laughed and laughed. "Everyone game is over now, let's go!" They all rushed to the classroom. After eight hours, the school was over. " DISPERSAAAAL!" all the students shouted. Some came running through the corridores shouting and screeming like tarzans.

Hayam, Yuki and Akima went to their bus. In morning, they were all stangers to each other but now, it looks like they've been knowing each other for years. Even Akuma got comfortable with them. "Okay, So you are Hayami. Rare name!" Said Akuma with a little smirk on his cold face. "Yaaaaas!" Said Hayami as Yuki pulled her hairs. "Ours!"

"So what? You mind your own business!" Said Yuki.

"Oh, I never knew that you can also ever have your own business" said Akuma.

"Ooooooo! Nice comeback bro!" all the students shouted. "Same here! We also didn't think that you have a brain to run your own business" Said hayami. "Shut up!" Said Akuma while nawworing his eyes.

"Oh ok, sorry while interrupting when you were throwing trash out of your mouth!" replied Hayami.

"Oooohh myyy Goddd!" shouted all the students.

"You're dumb!" Said Akuma. "Ohhh!!!" students shouted again. "And if you are smart, you should know when to shut up!" Said Hayami as she turned back infront. "So the winner of this competion is Hayami!" A child stood up and announced. Yuki nudged her.

Akuma smiled. " Congratulations!" He whispered to himself.

Hayami's stop came and she got down. "Bye Yuki! Bye Guys!" Exclaimed Hayami. "Bye! See you", shouted everyone.

XI
Chapter 11

"Kiyomi!Come someone is here to meet you!" Exclaimed Hiroshi. "Coming Dad" Hayami said thinking who can come to meet her. As she walked in the living room, she saw Yuki standinh ther. "Oh hi Yuki! Dad, she's my new classmate or you can say my new friend. Come in!" Yuki smiled and bowed down to her father. Ththey both went to Hayami's room "Wow! your room is so dreaming just like your hairs!" commented Yuki. "Oh thanks, by the way your dress is looking very pretty" Hayami complemented as she picked up all the scrolls from the bed to make space for Yuki to sit. Suddenly, she heard a click noise behined her and as ahe turned back she saw that Yuki locked the door.

"What's the need of that Yuki?" Hayami said as she got a bitnervous. She gulped and stared deep into Yuki's eyes. Within a few seconds, Yuki who was few centimeters smaller than Hayami got bigger. Her bro hairs turned into black. Her Green eyes went purple, she totally changed.

A sudden realizationhit Hayami that it wasn't Yuki but it was someone else in Yuki's get up to meet Hayami or even or even something else.

Hayami had been terrified plenty of times since leaving the orphanage where she grew up for one year. She'd thought nothing could ever be worsethan that moment when her beloved Aunt got killed by Queen right infront of her eyes.

This was a whale other level. "Who-Who- Who are-y-you?" Hayami flumbeled. "You don't know me? You've been living in my area for these many years and you don't know me?" That lady said in a hissy voice.

She didn't look that ugly or horrible but not also that pretty. Not bad but not good. "Her area?" Hayami thought. "Wait, Is it Queen splendour?" "Queen is it you?" She finally asked.

"Yes my child" Queen gave a weird look to her which made her feel a bit awkward. Hayami looked at her her in awstruck and said, "Why are you here and that also in my friend's get up?"

"Hayami dear, do you know? That which community do you belong? She asked. "No, but I also don't want to know". "Okay but, I wanted to tell you that you have some speacial powers!" Queen said that very slowly to make Hayami think over it and, she did. "Powers?!" She whispered in shock. "I have powers? Of what kind?"

"Eat this first". Splendour streched her hand with a handful of strawbwrries. "No! I can't my father has forbidden me from eating that". Hayami bursted out as she saw those. "You have to!" Queen took some starwberry and forcefully cramed them inside her mouth. Hayami scrumbled her eyes as she coughed two-to-three times. Not even a second passed when slowly- slowly Hayami's body started to turn into something. It was a-

DRAGON...

XII

Chapter 12

"Ahhhhh Mom!" Hayami yelled, but due to the soundproof room, her voice could'nt reach outside. She looked at herself in a mirror. Her scales, wings, her full body was looking so beautiful. Her scles were of bright colours like the birds of paradise. She had a prehensile tail and blue coloured shimmery eyes. She flexed her claws and then opened her mouth. "Oww!" She got scared by seeing her own sharp canines. "Your M-Majesty, I-I am- like wht's this?"

Splendour laughed at her reaction. "This is not only your power, you have many more ulterior," she said. "And one more thing, this power is common between your friends." Hayami looked at her in confusion. "My friends means w-who all?" Asked Hayami. "You, Akari, Hana, Toshiro and-" she gave a pause. "And?" Hayami questioned curiously. "Yuki and Akuma," she whispered in her ear slowly. "What?! They are not my friends yet we-, we just met today!" She explained. "Dear, the way others became your friend, they'll become too, just wait and watch." Queen said as if she can fortell the future. Hayami gave her a silent look while she flapped her wings. "And listen, you, Yuki and Akuma can spray DEATHVENOM from your hands."

"Oooo Fascinating! By the way is there any other powers which only I have, and no one else?" Hayami asked. "Yes! Listen to me carefully-

*You can breathe underwater for upto 2 hours.

*You can withstand subzero temperatures, and-"

She paused. "And what?" Hayami asked getting irritated from her habbit of stopping anywhere in betwenn of the conversation. "And you can do one more thing but only when you'll het the obsapphire stone."

"Obsapphire? What's that? And where is it found?" Asked Hayami as she loves exploring things. "Obsapphire is a gemstone which is a mixture of Sapphire and Obsidian. There are only 4 of them in our country. But, theres none of them in our community." Splendour said while making a clumsy face. Maybe becuase she was jealous of not having that precious stone in her kingdom. "So to find it do I-I have to go out of the kingdom?" Hayami asked nervously. "No!" Splendour rasped. "You can't even think to step out untill you complete your studies," she growled at her. "So-w- what's my p-power?" She asked. "You can-" The Queen paused again. Hayami sighed. "You can *read minds and fortell the future.*" She finally spoke. "Wow!" Hayami got a momentarily faint, imaging she could read minds and see that what's going to happen with her. Slowly-slowly, Queen Splendour turned back again to Yuki's getup and, *VANISHED...*

Hayami was shocked and happy at the same time. She sat on her bed and then...

CRAAAAAAAAAAAACK.....

Her bed broke. She forgot that she was still a dragon. When she got up, she slipped and stabbed her toe to a nearby table. The flower pot fell on her head. All the water poured down on her. "Ahh, it hurts!" She groaned. She scratched her head and then realized that she became normal. "Oh! So if I eat strawberries, I'll become a dragon, and when I'll pour water on myself, I'll be back to normal!" She laughed at herself.

"Rrrawwrgh!" She roared like a dragon while looking in a mirror.

XIII
Chapter 13

"But this is not safe" Hayami wake up ang got a flashback of yesterday's evening. "This is totally opposite of safe!" "What is unsafe Kiyomi?" Hiroshiasked as her entered into the room.

"Dad, you know that-" Hayami thought about whether she should tell that to her father or not. She had never hidden anything from her dad, but she was also very nervous.

"Dad, yesterday there were some people who were throwing stones at a dog. I was very sad, but it's not safe right? All the animals, innocent animals, they are getting hurt for no reason!" Hayami let out a sigh. "Oh my kind little daughter. There are many good and many bad people. You should know who to be with and whom with not." Hiroshi pampered her hairs.

"Hmm, thanks Dad!" Hayami said quietly. "Now go brush your teeth and get ready for your school !" Said Hiroshi as he left. "Is being dragon good?" She whispered to herself. "Haaaw!!" She yawned and got up.

She got fresh, wore her uniform and got ready for school. She woke up a bit early today so she still had 10 minutes for her bus to come. "Dad, Mom" Hayami called in low and slow voice. "What's the matter my child?" Sayuri said. "Umm, what will be your reaction if you get to know that ,ummm, I can be a"

"Dragon?" Hiroshi interrupted. Hayami was too petrified to respond anyway. "How did my Dad got to know?!" She thought , "May be knows that I can be a dragon, that's why he doesn't let me eat strawberries. And now, he's wondering that if I found out that I can be one".

"Yes dad, a dragon" she paused, " yesterday I heared a story of a girl who can change herself to a dragon", she lied.

"Oh! we would probably be a little scared and a little happy. Scared because, then you would have very sharp canines. You could bite us off! And happy becausewe'll be proud that our daughter as some special abilities but, regretfully, YOU ARE NOT OUR DAUGHTER!"

Hayami was coming towards her mother to hug but then, she frowned and backed off. She started sobbing but, no one noticed. She picked her bag up and went out.

"Bye Mom! by Dad!" She said in an upsent trembling voice. "Bye my child" shouted Hiroshi.

She sat down. She was looking outside of the window, even though she ws not able to see anything because of her blurry vision caused by the tears. "You are not our 'Daughter'! I hate you! I love Aiko and Hinata more! You are no more than a guest for us!" all these words were echoing in her head which made her feel even more sad.

Finally, a drop of tear rolled down her cheek. The bus came to a halt. She remembered that it's Yuki's and Akuma's stop. She remembered all those moments all her friend had made with her on Monday. That new game which Akuma invented and all and all. She quickly wiped her tears and cleared her throat. "Hi Hayami!" Yuki terrified and stumbbeled. She quickly hugged Hayami.

"Bye!" Akuma's mother said Akuma waved his hand and got up. Hayami was feeling comforted when she got hugged by Yuki. "Hi Yuki! Hi Hayami!" Akuma said.

"H-Hi" Hayami muffled as Yuki was hugging her very tightly. "Hi!" Yuki let out a breath as she sat down. "I-I want to tell you something Yuki", Hayami said as her voice was heavy. "Ya sure! On monday also you were trying to tell me something Yuki said doubtfully.

"Umm, actually the thing is that", Hayami was getting too nervous to say. "That?" "Yuki I'm- I'm adopted".

XIV
Chapter 14

"It's true Yuki, I-I am adopted", she relieved herself with a long breath. "W-What?" Yuki fumbled. "Why didn't you tell me this before!"

"I-I was thinking myself that should I tell this to you or not", Hayami got scared that she will lose such a nice pure-hearted friend just because of her real parents. Akuma was staring at both of them as if a drama is going on. "You should have told me before! Atleast you could have shared your problems and sadness with me. You must have felt really bad when you would have got to know about this. Don't you believe me as your friend?" Yuki said in a worried manner. Hayami's face lightened. She felt her own anxiousnes melting down and realized that she was thinking to much. *"She may not take me seriously"*, Hayami thought. *"But she really does love me"*.

"I'm sorry" Hayami voice dropped to an urgent whisper. "But I swear, I was not going to hide this from you". Yuki smiled, "It's okay! Better late than never". They laughed squeakily. Akuma was looking at them in WHAT-IS-HAPPENING-HERE manner. "Ahem-Ahem. Guys? You know what 'Laughter is the best medicine' but if you laugh for no reason, YOU MAY NEED A MEDICINE". Yuki and Hayami started laughing again. Akuma sighed. "Hayami! I've got an ice-cream you need?" Akuma asked joyfully. "Oh sure, thanks!" Hayami said grabbing it from his hand. "I need one too!" Yuki remarked. Akuma glared at her. "I said AN ice-cream. AN!"

"Wait! Yuki you can eat from the top and I'll eat from the bottom", Hayami said while tearing the packet apart. Mouth dry, stomach lurching Yuki said, "Okay! Nice idea!" They both started licking it. "Akuma, would you like to joing our friends group?" Yuki asked slyly as she saved one drop of that 'Almost Melted Ice-cream' from falling on her school uniform. "Friend? Me?" Akuma said as he gulped down. "Yes! Friend! You!" Hayami said in a childish manner. "No- I mean yes- umm -actually I've neaver made a friend before", he said while looking a bit dull. "Why is it so?" Yuki asked.

"When I was of 4-5 years old, my mother and father left me, and told me that I can only return back untill I earn some money for them. So then I started working as bodyguard. Even though I was young I was a really nice one. As I told you before, I have a lot of powers, they only helped me to achieve the title of the best bodyguard", he let out a sigh. "I got a lot of money like a-a billions but my parents took it. Not all, I still have some lakhs with me". Hayami and Yuki were astonished. "Now also you do that job?" Asked Yuki. "No! I don't do that job, but yes, I still do one", he replied. "Which one?" Hayami questioned. "I can't tell you that! I told you na IT'S MY COMMUNITY BUISNESS!"

XV
Chapter 15

"Oh okay, relax!" Yuki said. "By the way who was the first person of whom you became a bodyguard of?" Hayami asked quickly. Akuma's face went pale. He gulped down as he spoke, "It was a small girl. She was one-year younger than me. I don't remember her name. She used to call me Amigo! Her parents used to work outside the whole day, so they told me to become her bodyguard. As she was not a baby anymore, they didn't call a babysitter. I was of 5 that time. She was not just my boss but also my friend. She always treated me like one. And ya, she had a macaw as her pet. She had named her umm- I guess so-umm ya! SHE HAD NAMED HER MURIEL", Akuma exclaimed. Hayami tilted her head. "I guess that I've heard this name somewhere before", Hayami said looking confused. Yuki gaped. "By the way, do you know? That when I was of 4 years old, I had a bodyguard!" Hayami said trying to remember something. "Wow! Actually?" Yuki asked surprisingly. "Yeah, I don't remember properly because, when my actual parents left me in the orphanage, they had done some operation related to my brain. They had erased all my memory, that's why

I don't even remember the face of my adopted parents properly. My adopted mother, Mrs. Sayuri Yamaguchi told me about him. Guess he must be nice", Hayami said.

"Hayami you know what?" Akuma said. "That girl, of whom I became a bodyguard of also had blue hairs like you", Akuma said. "Seriously!? I thought that only Hayami have these blue-coloured magical hairs", Yuki said. The bus came to a halt as it reached. All the students started rushing. "Wow Yuki! See a macaw! It's so beautiful", Hayami said. "Wow, wonderful! Now tell me, why do you think everything is so very exciting?" Yuki said. Hayami felt lost. "I don't know, I just find everything so beautiful especially birds", she said smiling. Yuki snarled at her. They all reached the corridor. "Today you'll sit with me Hayami!" Akari shouted through the corridor. "Ya sure!" Hayami replied. "Yuki can sit with Hana today!" "Okay!" Yuki called back.

They all reached and kept their bags on their respective places. "Akuma! You can sit with me today", Toshiro said as he stumbled near the bench. "Umm-I-I prefer to be alone but-"

"Tsk, learn to be with others, or else you'll not get to fit properly in this school", Akari said. "Okay", Akuma went and sat down beside Toshiro. Yuki and Hana were sitting infront of Hayami and Akari, and Toshiro and Akuma were sitting behind them.

"Who's that?" Hayami spoke as she saw a women in a black dress outside the glass door. Everybody turned back and saw. "No one is there!" Akari said. The women had disappeared. Hayami looked in confusion. They all began talking again. Hayami saw Akuma was looking out of the door. Suddenly his face went purplish-dizzy. "Wait a second guys, I'm coming", he said as he ran outside. Hayami felt something fishy. She went behind him. She went near the door and tried to hear. "What have you observed till now?" Hayami guessed it was that lady's voice. "Nothing much but, got to know about their present queen and their old one. And yeah! I know all about your target's power", and this as Akuma's voice according to Hayami, deep, cold, and fierce. "You silly tiny little BRAT! I gave you only one job and you couldn't even do that properly?!" That unknown lady shouted. "My mission is not complete, it's true", said Akuma. "But I ensure you that you'll get what you want".

"Oh yeah?" That lady coughed wetly. "I'll see, my hopes are high with you, if you passed, WELL DONE! You'll get whatever you want and if you failed- WELL YOU ARE DONE THEN!" She growled at him. Akuma spread his hands and bowed deeply towards the lady. As, he glanced under his hand, his eyes met Hayami's. Akuma smirked. "Okay my majesty, I'll see you!" He said as he got up. "Okay! I'm going to. Take this paper", she said handing a piece of old paper to Akuma. The lady disappeared. It was were foggy there and due to that, Akuma and Hayami started to cough. Akuma muffled his hands on Hayami's face and said. "Don't tell what happened here to anyone or else, we both are going to be dead in SECONDS!" He growled. He released his hands.

"But who was that lady?" Hayami asked. "That's none of your concern!" Akuma said angrily. "I'll tell you everything afterwards but please, for now please don't tell what happened her to anyone. Or instead face the consequences that lady will do to all of us", he said in panik voice. Hayami nodded. He pushed her away as he entered into the class, as if she was just a tiny bloodsucking insect. They went inside.

XVI
Chapter 16

"Where did you guys disappeared?" asked Hana, "No where, I just wnet to walk outside that's al!" Said Hayami. "And I went to style my hairs," said Akuma. The teacher came in the class. "Gooooood Mooornni-" "SILENCE!" Yurie shouted. "Why did she got well, it was better when she was sick" Yuki whispered to Hayami. "You! stand up!" Yurie poined towards Yuki. Yuki gulped. She thought maybe the teacher overheared them.

"You're new right? Come here to my desk" "Ma'am but why? I've not done any-" " I just need some details" Yurie answered.

"And you also, the one sitting with Toshiro!" She enlargen her eyes at hi thinking he'll also get scared of her like others. He didn't say anything and went towards her Yurie ,Akuma and Yuki were gathered near the desk. She sat down. Yurie was asking some information like mother's name, father's name, blood groups etc,. "Ssh....Toshiro!" Hayami whispered." Can you please passs me the paper kept in Akuma's desk?"

"This one?"Toshiro took out a paper which looked very vintage and looked as if it was dipped in coffee. "Yes! And please promise me you won't tell him that I have this," she said as she snatched it. "Okay, I won't tell, promise" Toshiro said doubtly. Hayami threw that paper in her desk.

Yuki smiled at Hayami as she was talking to the teacher . Hayami also gave her a nervous smile. She drank water with her hands trembling. After sometime Akuma and Yuki came back to their places. Yuki smiled at Hayami which comforted her.

"Who can be that?" she thought. The first three periods were of History, Science and Biology. It was break time now. The bell trilled. Hayami quickly took the paper and ran to the restroom. She looked the door and opened the letter. It was as follows :

To - Akuma Kashiwagi

From - Queen Yasha

I'm starting to see why you're so useless! Don't you thinkthat I don't know what's going on. My daughter had told me that you are actually conspiring with the enemy. She told me that you are trying to make friends . Look! I'r telling you, be like how you were before, we want, - especially I WANT my cold, dark, mafia and bold ASSASSIN BACK! I hope you are loyal to me, if so, I'll make you ROYAL. As royal as no one. Hope, I'll see you again. You have to come here for teo- three days next week. We're planning to get the training for all the children. Osprey is already ready, remember? He was your past competitor. So we'll begin with you two. This time you gotta try to kill each other. Hope, you'll come prepared and our secret should not be leaked. It should be ulterior.

All the best

- Queen Yasha

Hayami gasped and gulped. "So , it means th- that, Ak-Akuma is a -a assassin?" She wishpered to herself. "HAVE YOU DIED INSIDE ! What's taking her so long ?" A girl shouted outside. "Coming !" said Hayami and she flushed so that she could think that she wasn't doing something suspicious. She came out and she kept that paper in her pocket. Hayami rushed towards the class.

By the time she reached ,the break was over.

As soon as she was about to enter in the class, she saw something crawling on the ground and when she went near it she saw it was a snake.

XVII
Chapter 17

She shoved herself back up dizzy, and disoriented. Hayami had got bitten by a Viper. She looked dazed.

" Hayami !" Akari, and Hana shouted as they came running out of the classroom. "Toshiro ! Akuma ! Yuki ! Come fast ! Akami called. Those two sat down and started rubbing her ands and feet. Yuki, Toshiro and Akuma came runnig. "NO!" Yuki yelled , "Hayami !"

"Stay back Yuki ! The Viper is still alive!" Toshiro shouted. Yuki and Akuma quickly came near Hayami, whereas Toshiro was blocked by the snake. He can't come forward or else, it would have bitter him too.

"Hayami! " Yuki started to cry. "Please don't die!" "Ow" Hayami said, trying to sit up. "Ow, I- my leg - wow, that actually really hurts - " She pressed her hands to her head and looked as if she might pass out.

"Hayami, I order you not to die," Akari said. Her normally bossy voice was full of panic. "Hayami, STOP IT! Stop dying RIGHT NOW!" Akuma said in a worried trembling voice. Blood started dripping out of her leg.

"Toshiro! Think! How do you stop a Viper's poison? The scrolls must have said something," Hana said. "Um - Why can't I remember anything ? Why is that spreading so fast ?" Toshiro muttered as he saw Hayami's face was turning slowly- slowly white.

"You can't die!" Akuma yelled at her. "I won't let you!" Akuma sat down as he hit the ground and a slid near her. "What - are y- you going to do? " Yuki started forward. "Anything for my friend" he said quietly. "Us too!" everybody shouted. Akuma kept his hand on her leg. Nearly stabbed her.

With a roar of crazed agony, Hayami surged up. "Hayami, it's alright we all are trying to help you!" Hana comforted, but Hayami was in too much painto hear her. She jerked and thrashed. A purple coloured substance came out of Akuma's hand which stopped the crazy flooding of blood. "What-how-how-did-why-you did t-that?" Akari asked nervously. "Just using my powers", he was applying full pressure on that bite. "But how can a snake come in the school?" remarked Toshiro. "Guess I know that who did that", Akuma said angrily. Each second he was applying more and more pressure. "Ahh, Guys! Please you also come and apply pressure on it with me!" Akuma said. Everybody kept their hands on his hand and applied full pressure. Suddenly a blue neon light came out. "I'm not sure she can survive this", Hana whispered gentaly. "She can!" Yuki exclaimed. "Definetly! She can!" Said Akari. "Mayabe no one else can but, *she can*", Akuma said fiercly. Hana saw the teachers coming. "Just do whatever your'e doing, fast, but just make sure that she'll get good", Akari said in panick. "I'm trying!"

"Okay guys, leave all of your hands in 3..2..1.. LEAVE!" Akuma said immediatly. All of them fell behind. Yuki got up and said, "Hayami? Are- are you alright?" Akari looked at her in concern. "I think she is, I don't see that wound anymore, do you?" Toshiro got up and stared. "That's all of it", Akuma said in an exhausted voice. "Is she alright? Tell me that it worked!" Akuma said his voice rising. Hayami had passed out. "It worked!" Hana and Toshiro said happily.

XVIII
Chapter 18

"What's happening here?" Yurie came shouting. "Ahhh! SNAKE!" The coordinator shouted. Yurie stared at it in horror. "Ma'am Hayami's got bitten by a snake," a random child shouted. "What? Sister ! Take her to the nurse!" Said Yurie. "Ah - thanks g- guys, Ah- m- my head!" Said Hayami.

"Hayami! I was so worried for you," Yuki said happily. "Aww, I'm feeling good now Yuki. I mean not that good" Hayami said. "Are you alright?" Akuma asked with guilti n his voice as he realized that he had been too much oppresive with her in the morning. "Hmm" Hayami replied. "I'm not feeling that well n-now," Hayami struggled to sit. And then she lapsed back into unconsiousness. Two nurse came and took he to the sick- bay. "How can a snake come in our school?!" Coordinator shouted.

Akuma ran from their in the class. He searched that letter in his desk but, no sihn of it. "Hey Toshiro! Have you seen any letter or paper kept in my desk?"

Toshiro gulped looking washed out. "Um, No, I haven't seen any paper." Akuma narrowed his eyesat him. "Um, okay yes, I know, Hayami has that." "What! who gave that to her?!" Akuma asked furiously. "It was me,"Toshiro looked down in shame.

"You! I think I'll deal with you later." Akuma rushed to sick- bay. "May I come in nurse? Akuma asked crippling. "Yes, you may" the nurse said when she was writing somthing in her register. Akuma went near Hayami and started searching all her pockets. Finally he found that letter in her skirt pocket and then he sat on a chain and opened it. He read it all. "Oh God! If Hayami had not read this it's pretty good but, if she has then - she would have known that I'm an -

ASSASSIN!" he whispered in panick. He ran from there so that he won't get late for the lecture. "Look who has came!" Yurie shouted. "You have bunked the class."

"I'm sorry ma'am. I did n -,"

"What sorry? Where were you?" Yurie bellowed. Akuma found an excuse, "Ma'am I was with Hayami in the sick-bay."

"Okay, settle down", Yurie said embarresly. "I'm sorry Akuma", Toshiro said. "Fine" Akuma snarled coldly at him. "I've never met a child more pointless than you." He sat down as he pushed the chair behind fiercly to make space to sit.

"How is Hayami?" Yuki asked sadly. "You met her right?" asked Akari. "Ya, I met her and- um- she's fine resting with the healers."

"*Why is Queen Yasha so restless ?*" Akuma thought . "May be she's afraid of the powers I have." He smiled at himself. "And maybe Hayami's powers too", he whispered. "Akuma? You alright?" Toshiro asked. "Yeah, just feeling very tired", Akuma said with a ghost of smile on his face.

That day, in evening when the Queen splendour had visited Hayami's house in Yuki's getup and told about all the powers she has, that day in the evening only, Akuma had used his powers. And it was MIND- READING-

He knows everything about Hayami's, Yuki's, Toshiro's and Akari's powers as HE HAD READ HER MIND.

XIX
Chapter 19

He knew that Hayami, Yuki and he can become a dragon. He knew that their trio (Hayami, Akuma and Yuki) can shoot death venom from hand. He actually knew that Hayami can -

*Breath underwater for upto two hours

*Can withstand subzero temperatures

*Spray death venom

*Read minds and

*Fortell the future...

Basically, the last two were only possible if she could get the obsapphire stone. "What's wrong with my Queen?" Akuma was thinking hard. His first guess was that his community wanted ti use Hayami's, Yuki's and his deathvenom themselves as, it was one of the most powerful weapons in Philia. If they could somehow replicate the venom or adapt it for their own purposes, that plus their telepathy and precognition would make his community UNSTOPPABLE. But the main reason, his community wanted to attack on this, DIAMOND COMMUNITY was because they needed a new place to stay. They wanted to capture Philia's top. A new home for his community to stay, safe and peaceful. But is it going to be possible now?

"Hayami knows about Queen Yasha and about what I really am!" Akuma thought. "If this secret will become a topic to discuss among, that will doom everyone to a horrible end!"

"May I-I come i-in ma'am?" Hayami came limping as her leg was still hurting. "Yes sure! Are you all good now?" Yurie asked botherly. "Yeah almost", she said slowly. Akari came and helped her to settle at her place. Yuki cheerfully looked at her and held her hand, under the bench. "Say thanks to Akuma, he's the one who has saved your life", Akari said. But Hayami was totally lost in her thoughts, she had many queries which she could share with Yuki, but can get the answer only from Akuma.

"Of which community is Akuma from? Queen Yasha is the queen of which community? Is Akuma actually an assassin? If he is, so why did he saved her life? How can a snake come in their school? And why did Akuma say that he knows, that who had send the snake in the school? Why did that mysterious Queen Yasha said that Akuma was conspiring with the enemies?" And many more.

"Akuma how did you save Hayami's life? I mean a viper's poison is way too deadly to be survivable!" Toshiro asked Akuma in a low voice. "I just did and yeah, it was kinda hard", Akuma said looking at that letter. "Which community are you from?" Toshiro asked. "I don't know", he replied. "I don't think so that your'e from this Diamond community because, the people of this community are very kind-hearted and caring. You are also okay like, you saved Hayami's life today but, if we exclude thta, not only me, but almost everyone thinks that you are very ruthless and way too cold", Toshiro remarked thinking he will get angry on him. "It's okay, haven't you heard that quote? DOGS WILL BARK!"

The bell rang and then all went to their buses...

• 53 •

XX
Chapter 20

"Hayami, will you come to the diamond delta park today evening? Only if you are okay", Akari asked. "Yes! Sure! I can", Hayami called back. "Is there any one else coming?"

'I can come!" Yuki exclaimed. "Maybe I also can", said Akuma looking a bit tensed. "I have to ask my parents", said Toshiro. "I am coming! I guess", Hana said. "Okay so almost everyone are coming right?" Akari asked. "Yaaaas!" Everyone shouted. Hayami smiled. Everyone went to their respective buses. Today in the whole bus ride, Hayami was not talking to Akuma. "What happened Hayami? Why aren't you and Akuma talking?" Yuki asked innocently. Hayami looked at her with doe eyes. "Should I call him?" Yuki said half turned back. "Nooo!!! Please!" Hayami said quickly. "Why?!" Yuki said in a little raised voice. "Absolutely not! It's just I'm not feeling well that's why," said Hayami panickly as she thought Yuki will tell Akuma that she wanted to talk to him. Hayami's stop came and she got down.

"Sister! Why are you looking so pale?" Hinata came running to her. "Nothing just - just a snake bit me", Hayami replied quietly. "Mom! Dad! Quickly come here ! Aiko you too Hayami -" and the bus pulled away. Yuki and Akuma smiled seeing that family reunion on a bus stop. "Did you and Hayami fight ?" Yuki asked.

"No, the - there's nothing like that", Akuma replied, looking nervous for the first time. Their stop came and they got off.

IN THE EVENING -

"Oh Hi, you reached before me!" Akari shouted. Hayami slowly - slowly walked towards her. They had a hug. Suddenly, "Hi Hayami! " Yuki came sprinting. they all gathered. "Okay listen, Hana won't be able to come", said Akari.

"Her family has gone out to a function." "Oh, now what to play?" Yuki asked. "Aaha! Toshiro came too!" Hayami said. "Hey! Akuma didn't arrive?" Toshiro asked looking here and there, everywhere. "Not yet", said Akari. "Now what do we do ?" Akari asked everyone.

"Maybe play that recreate the history game again? How is - "

"No! " Everybody shouted. "Then maybe hide and seek" Yuki suggested. "Let's do something for Hayami as she's not well. We can umm - " said Toshiro. "Ya nice idea but what can we do ? sing a song?" remarked Akari.

"Actually", said a new voice, "I have a better offer." Hayami whirled around as a person in black t- shirt, black cargo, black mask and in black jacket descended from the gate and gave her a cheeky grin. "Hello, Hayami", said Akuma.

XXI
Chapter 21

"Akuma! You came!" Toshiro yelled. "Savage dress! Nice", Akari commented. Yuki just smiled and then looked at Hayami, who looked exasperated. Akuma's gaze was stuck on her as he was thinking how can he make it up to her.

"Okay let's everyone settle down first!" Said Yuki. They all found a place to sit. It had a roof made of grasses of leaves and flowers. "Ya so, what was your offer? " Asked Yuki. "I can tell a story, and it's not at all that boring, its very interesting", said Akuma still looking at Hayami. Finally she spoke, "Don't give me that smug face!" She snapped.

"This isn't my smug face, it's my heroic face", Akuma said looking a bit happy as she spoke to him. "Hang on ! I have rescued you , because of me you are alive!" Akuma said as he stood up. "They both are one of the best savage repliers, if they both ever fought, the world might blast!" Akari whispered to Yuki and Toshiro.

"Aren't you pleased?" Said Akuma as he stepped forward. He plucked a stick from the bushes. "This will be my mic!" Said Akuma cheerfully. "You deserve this only!" Hayami replied. Akuma thought, *"Desrve what? This wooden mic or her not talking to me?"*

"Sensible girl", said Akuma. He gave Hayami an unreadable look - teasing but worried, and self - satisfied and sweet all at once. He sat down infront of his friends and wore that hoodie on.

"Ahem- Ahem so hello guys, today, I, Akuma Kashiwagi is going to articulate a story. I will just speak whatever comes in my mind okay? And this story is for Hayami."

XXII

Chapter 22

Once upon a time there was a girl named - Poppy. She loved animals. I mean a lot. She always wanted a rabbit but she couldn't get one. She was in grade 6th and was very good in studies. Now -a- days she was really very happy as her birthday was about to come in few days. She was really very excited and started toying with the idea. She planned a birthday party at home.

Few days later -

Finally that day came. Poppy woke up in the morning and got freshed up. When she walked across her house, she saw that no one was there.

"Mom! Dad! Where are you! Please don't leave me, I'm scared!" She cried.She started to find them outside but no sign of them. She sat on her swing for two-three hours, just crying and missing her parents. Suddenly she heard a voice,

a voice of someone squeaking,

was it a -

Yes it was! It was a rabbit. She gaped and took that rabbit in herarms. Her mom and dad came back home. "Mom! where did you both go? By the way see! I foundsuch a beautiful rabbit!" She said suprisingly. "That's your birthday gift my child!" Her dad said.

"Thanks daddy, thanks mom!" She named the rabbit 'Socket'.

She had a really nice party in the evening. Many of her friends had also arrived. They ate a delicious, mouth - watering choco - strawberry cake and many more. Poppy had a really nice day.

But then, few weeks later she saw that socket was looking very sad. She asked her father about it and he said that socket might be ill. Poppy used to be very sad. She thought that being ill was not a good thing and god has done really bad to her rabbit.

She used to ask her neighbours, friends, shopkeepers etc., that how can socket become well like before, but no one knew anything. But one day, she met a shopkeeper who told her about a fairy. He told that there is a fairy who stays at the top of the snowy mountains. She might have a solution for poppy's rabbit.

Poppy was very happy. She started hiking on the snow mountain. It took days and days to reach there, finally she reached. She told herself, "Poppy don't be scared. Socket will be alright.

Always remember that -
The mountain is very high,
It's tall and touches the sky
About the mountain, the people will only talk,
But only the real BRAVE reaches the TOP...

She saw a hut and went in there. It was very beautiful from inside. She saw a very pretty fairy sitting on a carpet, wearing a petite flower crown. Poppy told that fairy about her problem. "Oh I see!" The fairy said as bold as could be. "I know onw thing that can cure your rabbit it's that you have to find a hat." "A hat? That's very easy!" Poppy cheered. "But you can only have the hat of a person who has never fallen sick." "Never fallen sick?!" Poppy thought.

She bowed to the fairy and went. "I need a hat!" Poppy asked the shopkeeper "Ya sure!" He brought a hat and gave it to poppy. "Thank you but wait, have you ever fallen sick?" She asked. "Umm, yes! I had got dengue, " he replied and Poppy frowened. She met many people but she couldn't find anyone who has a hat and had never fallen sick. One day she sat on her swing with her rabbit on her lap. She thought and thought.

Then - she realized what the fairy actually meant! She wanted to teach Poppy that , there's no one who has never fallen sick. Socket, her rabbit is not alone. Being sick is a part of life from whom, everybody undergoes.

From that day she started taking care of Socket preciously. Then one day when she woke up in the morning - BOOM ! She saw that Socket was cured. She was very happy and they lived happily ever.

XXIII

Chapter 23

"Wow!" said Yuki. "Amazing!" said Akari. "I can't believe you have made that!" Remarked Toshiro. "Thanks guys ", Akuma said but still he wasn't that happy as Hayami didn't praise or said anything about him or his story. Everyone looked at Hayami.

Her eyes, they were full of tears. "Hayami, are you okay?" Yuki asked and then she hugged her. It was a pretty fierce one. She started to cry. Everyone gathered around her and tried to comfort her. "My story wasn't that emotional !" Akuma said. "I'm not crying because of the story!" Hayami cutely protested.

"I'm just thinking how lucky I am for for having such god-gifted friends like you all", she sobbed. "Awww", Akari said. Toshiro gave her a napkin. She wiped her tears and coughed. Akuma bought a water bottle and gave to her. Yuki snatched it from his hand and slowly-slowly made Hayami drink it. "Okay I've got a joke, Why do the pirates take so long, to learn the ABC's?" AKari asked. "Maybe cause they're illitrate?" Yuki guessed. "Mayabe?"

"Hayami will tell us the answer", Akari whispered cheerfully. Hayami looked at her with teary doe eyes. "It's becuase t-they have spent their whole life on th C", she said childishly. Everybody started laughing. Yuki laughed so hard that she had to take the support of the bench to stand properly. Everybody got happy seeing Hayami laughing. Hayami giggled. "I want to talk about something with Akuma, personally", Hayami said. "It's alright, you can express your undying gratitude to me later or even now also. I'll listen", Akuma said teasingly. "I'm serious bro!" Hayami said coldly. "Okay girl, go easy! Tell me what's the matter", Akuma said. Hayami kept quiet. "EVERYBODY GET OUT!" Akuma shouted. All the other three got out shivering after hearing Akuma's thuner voice. "Hayami! Tell me that secret afterwards too!" Yuki said cheerfully as she was walking out. Hayami smiled at her. Everybody hae gone. "Tell me now", Akuma said as he sat down beside her. "Who. Is. Queen. Yasha?!" She yelled. "She's Queen obviously!" Akuma giggled. "Tell me Akuma, I'm not joking!" Her voice rised."Okay I'll tell you but promise you won't tell it to anybody", Akuma warned. Hayami nodded.

"She's the Queen of our community", said Akuma.

"What's your community?"

"I-It's NIGHTPOWERS" Akuma said lowly.

"I've never heard it before!" Hayami said curiously.

"Ya, that's obvious because it's underground!" Akuma said.

"Okay so you mean it's a secret community? I can't understand anything, explain it to me from starting, you're making everything so obfuscate", Hayami said. Akuma let out a breath.

"Okay so-

I'm from a community named NIGHTPOWERS. It's an underground secret community about no one knows about. I-I am an assassin. Queen Yasha, the Queen of our community has send me here so that I can spy and give her information. She wants to invade in the Diamond community because she wants her kingdom to see the outside world.

Our community used to be outside many years ago. But when other communities united, they ordered us to go, so we went underground. Queen Yasha just wanted revenge. She's going or you can say planning to attach on this community.

Not now, may be years after. But she will. He relieved a long suffering sigh. "Ooo fascinating! But I still can't believe that you are an assassin",said Hayami. "You have to believe that. But why do you think that I'm not?" Asked Akuma. "You didn't kill but you saved my life!"

"Ya, because you are my friend !" Said Akuma as he smiled. "Okay, I have one more question, can you become a dragon?" "Hayami, I know that Queen Splendour had visited your house few days ago in evening. And let me tell you, I can read minds." Akuma said. "You can read minds?" Hayami gasped.

"Yeah, so basically -

"I had read your mind that day and I know about all your powers as well as that You, I, Yuki, Toshiro and Akari can become a dragon."

XXIV
Chapter 24

"Oh, so you know everything about me?" Asked Hayami. "Yes", replied Akuma. " So, um - do you know anything about that news?" Hayami whispered. "Which news?" Akuma said. "That missing people of Rain birds community?"

"Oh, that one! Yes, I even know that who have taken them", Akuma said. "Really? Who did that?!" Hayami asked. "Osprey, he's my brother, he's Queen Yasha's take carer. Many years ago, Rain birds used to trade the fruits and vegetables with night powers gems, emeralnd etc., But when the night powers went underground, they started to realize that they don't have enough food for their kingdom.

When they requested the Rain birds to give them an underground supply for food, and in return, they'll get gems, they denied and not only that, they've also insulted our community alot for being the most useless and weak commuity.

"So, Queen Yasha has decided to kidnapp the Rain birds slowly - slowly and then in return of those people . The Rain birds will have to give them a nice food supply." "Seems like queen Yasha is so clever!" Hayami nudged him. They giggled.

"And now one last question then I'll let you go", said Hayami. "Okay ask me", Akuma said as Hayami moved a little she saw someone's shadow near that place. Akuma saw it too. "Which tiny little creature is trying to listen our talks?" Hayami called.

Then she heard someone laughing and then the shadow disappered. "By hearing the sound of laugh I think so its Yuki," said Hayami. "Me too! Akuma said cheerfully.

"Okay now tell me, who had sent that snake in our school? I swear I'm going to bite the person's head off and stuff him in a volcano!" Hayami roared. "Since that's kind of already happened. I mean, that volcano part. Today afternoon, I've got a news that Smolder was trying to fry his chips to make it crunchy while sitting on a volcano. And suddenly, splaaaaaash. He fell into the lava. Yeah 'smolder' had sent a snake to kill you", said Akuma

"Is he a kind of pschyo or something? Who fries chips on a volcano and wait, VOLCANO'S DO EXIST?" Hayami asked.

Yes, in Philia , volcano's do not exist. People have only heard about them in storiestha they are a mountain or a hill having a crater through which lava, rock, fragments, hot vapour and gas are or have been erupted from the Earth's crust.

"Yes, in Night powers underground community, volcanos do exist", relpied Akuma. "By the way, why did he want to kill me?" Hayami asked. "That's because Queen Yasha had ordered to kill you. She only wants me who has the power of becoming a dragon. That's why she wants to kill yoou." Akuma said. "But then why she doesn't want to kill Toshiro, Akari and ...Yuki?" Hayami questioned. "That's because - "

XXV
Chapter 25

"That's because they can only become a dragon. You have other powers as well. So you are more powerful then those three", Akuma said. "Was that a compliment?" Hayami asked. "No, it was an answer" said Akuma.

"By the way,um I- I am sorry for being too harsh with you today morning", said Akuma. "It's okay! But still I was a bit angry from you. And I still am a little", Hayami said quietly. "Umm okay you can take your time", Akuma. "You all can come inside!"Hayami shouted. They all came inside running. "Oh my legs!" Said Akari in tired voice. "We were standing outside since past ten minutes!" Toshiro yelled. "I'm so tired!" Yuki was exhausted. "Okay umm so, now what?" Akari

"Photo Time!" Yuki exclaimed. Hayami took out a camera from her pocket and they all posed. Yuki was hugging Hayami, Akari made a bunny behined both of themmwith fingers, Akuma held Yuki shoulder with one hand and with other he did a V - pose and Toshiro made a rockstar pose.

"Okay so let's go home then, Bye!" said Akari. "Bye!" everyone exclaimed and went to their homes. Hayami and

Yuki walked to the gate together. "You know what Yuki?" Said Hayami. "What?" Yuki said quietly. "You would actually look very cute if you were a dragon." "Huh? Dragon? Me?" Yuki said in confusion. "Yes! Dragon! You!" And they both laughed together and then everyone parted their ways.

"How was your day Hayami!" Aiko asked as Hayami was washing her hands. "Is youe fever okay?" Asked Sayuri. "Yes Mom, I'm fine and Ya, my day was very nice", replied Hayami. "What if, if you get high fever again?" Asked Hiroshi as he looked worried.

"God did very bad to my sista", said Hinata. "No dad, I'm fine and - Hinata, you should know this too that Being sick is a part of my life" Hayami smiled at her. " Okay let's go and have dinner", Sayri said. "And don't forget to have your medicine Hayami" said Hinata. They all happy went , had dinner, watched TV, laughed and slept.

XXVI
Chapter 26

Today, was holiday " Ahhhhh !!!" Hayami woke up out of fright. "MoooooM !!!" Hayami thought that it was Hinata's voice. She woke up and went out. "Moon! Hayami!"

Hayami heard this voice coming from the living room which was downstairs. "Why did she my name?" Hayami paniced. As As soon as she entered the hall,"Aaaaaaaa !!!" Everybody screeched so lound that Hayami held her ears. "What happened!" Hayami asked.

"Look at yourself!" Aiko said trembling. Hayami looked down. Her colourful scales shimmered. Her sharp talons were shining in the morning sunlight. "How is this possible?" Hayami whispered under her breath. "Did you eat strawberries Hayami? I told you not to eat them!" Hiroshi shouted.

"No Dad, I didn't eat any strawberry then how did this happen?" Hyami said nervously. "What do you mean by THEN? Did you know that you can become a dragon before before only?" Hiroshi asked. Hayami looked down in guilt. "Aaaaa!!!" Aiko screamed, looked at Hayami , and screamed again. "Yes Dad, I knew this from before only", Hayami said quietly. "This is Hayami?!" Sayuri said in frozen terror. "Dad! I think so, it's because of my -

SYRUP MEDICINE! Ya, I remember, they contained strawberries, rasberries, Thiamine Hydrochloride umm, - De - Dextromethorphan Hydrobromide and umm - " Hayami said counting the ingredients on her talons. Hiroshi sighed. "Sayuri, Aiko and Hinata please, I request you all not to tell this to anyone and specially , you Sayuri", Hiroshi said.

"Huh? What do you mean by specially me?" Sayuri widened her eye at him looking annoyed. "Hayami, you go and splash some water on yourself, you'll be fine, "Hiroshi said. Hayami ranto the terrace and jumped in the swimming pool. Splaaashhhh....

"Oh my clothes, there's so wet", Hayami said as she slowly came back to her room, tip -toeing. "Now my whole family knows about my beautiful scales, it's all because of my medicine!" She gotangry but cutely.

"Akari?" Hayami said softly as she saw her phone ringing. She picked it up. "Hi Akari, what happened ?" Hayami asked. "Haya - Hayami, umm - TO - Toshiro", Akari said fumbbling and trembling . "What happened to Toshiro?" Hayami asked as she got scared. "T - Toshiro is - KIDNAPPED"

XXVII
Chapter 27

"What! H-How? When?" Hayami said in horror." Her mother called me and told about it, she asked me whetherToshiro was at my home or not, I - I- What to do now?" Akari said in sorrow. "Umm - O- Okay, I'll see if I'll get to know anything about him or not" Hayami said in panic and then she hung up.

She quickly changed her clothes and then rushed to the dinning area. "Mom! Dad! Toshiro is missing ", Hayami said. "What? What happened? Who told you?" Sayuri asked. Hayami told her evrything from the phone call till she came running down the stairs. "Okay, I'll try to find about it", Hiroshi said.

They all ate their food their food. Hayami rushed to her room to call Toshiro mom and get to know more about it. "What's this? " Hayami said as when she entered the room she found a, scroll on her bed. "I never took a scroll out today", she said while looking at it.

It was in a golden as well as black colour. "Whoow! I've never seen such a golden coloured scroll in my library", she said surprisingly. She sat down and tried to open it.

"Password!" A weird kind of raspy voice came out of that. "Password? Do scrolls keep passwords?" Hayami said in shock. "Let's guess, is it umm - Diamond?"

"Incorrect", the voice came again. "Queen Splendour?" Hayami said confidently ."Wrong". "Let's try my name, uh - um, Hayami Yamaguchi?" "Correct!" The voice said. Hayami hesitated. Soon, the curled scrolled started to open by itself. Words started to flash out. All the words were written in a glossy shiny way. They were coming out of the scrolls.

Hayami touched those letters. "Wait, it seems like, this is - r- real diamond? Wow!" Hayami said. As soon as she started to read - "Hayami! I'll read it for you", said the raspy voice from the scroll. Hayami gave that scroll an extremely odd look. "Really?"

"Yes ! Ahem -Ahem -

To Hayami Yamaguchi

from Q - Queen Yas - Yasha,

Hi dear Hayami, you're so lucky, I mean more than that because you survived a- a VIPER'S ATTACK. That's a kind of cool, but we won't let you for survival! You mightbe asking that " who four?" Am I right! They are You, Yuki, Akari and Toshiro. So we thought of starting it from the last so, guess where Toshiro is? In my DUNGEON! So, if you wan't ...... alive, try to come and save him with your friends. You can ask about the loction from Akuma. Bye, see you in my kingdom!" The raspy voice coughed and the scroll closed.

"Toshiro is with Queen Yasha?" Hayami quickly went, picked her phone and called Akuma. "Hey Akuma,can you please - please - plleaaasse send me Queen Yasha's address?" Hayami begged. "Why do you want that?" He asked being amused. "Toshiro is in Queen Yasha's dungeon, please give me the address", said Hayami. "What? O - Okay but even if I give you that, you can't go there", Akuma said. "W- Why?

Why is it so?

"That's because is under Scorpian mountain and ,you know where is that", Akuma said. "It's outside of our community", said Hayami.

XXVIII
Chapter 28

A macaw came flying in her room. It chirped loudly as it sat on Hayami's head. "Wait- this is my bus friend macaw, THE ONE WHO ALWAYS MEETS ME IN THE BUS. He came here too?"

"Wait, keep quiet for a second", Akuma said immediatly. They both fell silent. "chrpp chrrp", the macaw chirped. "This voice is familiar to me", Akuma said thinking hard. "You also think that? Same here! It feels like, I mean, umm- like as if I have a really strong connection with this macaw", Hayami said looking dreamy. "Does that macaw has a cut above his right eye?" Akuma asked desperatly. Hayami patted that bird's head then slowly grazed her hand above his eye to look. He had a fine straight scar which went slight diagonal. "Umm-Yeah he has", Hayami said. "IT'S MURIEL!!!" Akuma cried in a cheerful voice. "Who? w-wait that name- I-I've heard it before", Hayami said.

"I told you na about that girl, of whom I became a bodyguard! Her pet macaw! MURIEL!" Akuma exclaimed. Hayami had never seen him so cheerful before. "Maybe he can take me to that girl. I-I wanted to talk to her. She's my first friend who I've ever got in my life!" Akuma said.

"Okay but wait, if Muriel is of that girl's, why is she not taking care of him, I mean, I've always seen this macaw wandering and flying here and there on the roades and skies", Hayami said. "And why is it coming to me all the time?"

Akuma felt silent. "H-Hayami?" He said is a low sobbing voice. "Yes?" Hayami said in a curious way. "You said that, when you were of f-four years, you had a b-bodyguard right? A-And you don't remember much about him a-as your parents erased all your memory before leaving you in an o-orphanage?" Akuma asked in a fast speed. "Yeah, I just remember him a little. Not much. I've forgetten everything. I just know a little about everyone I've met ever in my life. About my parents also. They were very good, I just don't remember their faces. Same with my that bodyguard too, I know a little things about him, but I don't remember his face", Hayami said is a low voice. "Y-Y-You" Akuma said as he was lacking his breath. "Hmm?" Hayami asked.

"YOU ARE THAT GIRL!! OF WHOM I BECAME THE BODYGUARD OF!" Akuma said finally with a excitment on his face. "W-What?" Hayami asked as she got shocked. "Yes! I was your bodyguard! And you know why this macaw is coming to you all the time? That's because that you may have forgetten everything, but he hasn't. HE IS YOUR PET MACAW!" Hayami looked at that macaw. Suddenly her head went round and round. The macaw was staring into her eyes, and she was too. As they made an eye-contact, Hayami started to remember something. All her moments with her macaw, playing, singing, eating, sleeping, which she loved the most. When Hayami looked deep into his eyes, she started seeing his feelings. Macaw's eyes were full of tears. Though, they didn't fell on the ground but it seemed like someone is stopping the overflow of the tank of at least a thousand liters. Hayami quickly hugged that macaw tightly. "Thank you, *MY AMIGO!*" Hayami said happily. Extremely happily. Akuma smiled. He was also very happy after he finally found out that her friend is okay. "By the way Akuma, if you were my bodyguard then it's obvious that you would know that who my parents are?" Hayami asked as an thought popped in her mind. "Yeah! I clearly remember their faces and I also know that where they are", Akuma said. "Where?" Hayami asked. "The place where Toshiro is. In the dungeon".

XXIX
Chapter 29

"WHAT? THI-THIS CAN'T BE!" Hayami shouted her voice shaking. "Yes, so probably, we can save them also if we went to save Toshiro", Akuma said. "So what to do now?"

"So we escape?" Hayami asked doubtfully. "Just like all my friends and I wanted. We escape tonight. Right now!" Akuma kept quiet. "Escape?" He squeaked. "Seriously?" Akuma's voice changed again to the dark cold one. "Don't need to act cold infront of me! I know you from childhood", said Hayami. "Okay but, you don't have to do anything. I guess if I ask my old classmates in the NIGHTPOWERS community, we can manage. We'll fight her or umm- figure something out..."

"Ofcourse we have to do something!" Hayami said fiercly. "If escape was actually that easy, we, or you all would have done it already!" Akuma said. "Yeah, you've got that point", Hayami replied. "Okay so, the secret we had, can we share it to all the rest of us, I mean the rest four of us?" Hayami asked. "Huh? You've again lost the terror of our powers? Why aren't you fumbling?!" Akuma chuckled. "Shut up! Now tell me, my question still stands". Akuma wasn't saying anything. Hayami thought that if he would have been infront of her, he would make a cold face and stare at her in anger. "Okay but make sure it stays only between the six of us, if anybody else got to know about this, I AM DEAD! But I have a condition for that", Akuma said."What? Condition? Tell me", Hayami said dauntlessly. "You have to be my friend again", Akuma said. "Bruh! We were friends when we were under five, but did we break our friendship when we got seperated, or when I went to orphange?" Hayami said. "Okay but still FINE! Condition accepted".

Akuma smiled as they hung up the call. Hayami called everyone and told them about everything. "I can become a dragon?" Yuki said innocently but with horror. "What the heck-? I-I'm a dragon?" Akari said. Hayami got many weird and awkward sayings from them all. Finally she told everyone about their plan which was that,-

THEY'LL ESCAPE TONIGHT...

XXX

Chapter 30

"WATER BOTTLES!"

"Check!"

"10 PROTEIN BARS!" Hayami asked

"Check!" Akari replied.

All the five of them had assembled at Hayami's house. Yuki brought a 3 bags, which they all will carry on their backs. Properly. "THREE CLOTHES FOR EACH OF US WHICH MEANS, 18 CLOTHES?!"

"Check", Akari said as she kept looking at the objects while Hayami ticked on a paper where all the list of the items were written. "I'm first only telling you, t-this is a terrible idea!" Yuki said. Akuma looked at her and said "It will be alright bro! Chill!" Akari laughed at her fear. Yuki pouted.

They all had planned to start walking at night eleven, when almost everyone is asleep, especially Queen Splendour. They would dig the mountain hole as much as they can. I would take approx two hours to do that. Then they'll enter in the outside world, finally Hayami will be able to do what she had ever dreamt in her whole life.

Exploring out, meeting her parents was just brilliant. Then they'll probably describe themselves as Queen Yasha's typicall assassins, which were sent to the Diamond community to kill them. Akuma told that the soldiers in the Nightpowers community were way too foolish. So, they would probably get into their lie thinking it is truth and let them inside. Akuma, as he is the assassin, he has full righ t to kill anyone but specially on orders. He will kill the guards infront of the dungeon and then they will get Toshiro out and Hayami, SHE'LL FINALLY MEET HER PARENTS... But things were not that easy as she thought. There were many people around there who are dying to KILL THEM.

"Packing done!" Yuki said. "Now see we have to be ready as soon as we can, it's already nine", Akuma said. "Children! come down dinner time!" Sayuri shouted. All of them came running down the stairs. They all settled down and started stuffing their food in their mouth. "Why are you all eating like this?" Hiroshi commented. "Nothing just, we have to complete our school project as fast as we can, even Toshiro is also not there with us right?" Hayami said as she inserted a bite of Mochi in her mouth.

"Oh yeah! Got to know anything about Toshiro yet?" Hinata asked as her head was above the table and rest of her body, under it. She was almost peeping above to eat. "No, no yet", Akari said as she smiled at Hinata's cuteness. Hinata showed her shiney white teeth back. Hayami started eating slowly. "Why are you eating so slowly?" Yuki asked Hayami in an urgent low whisper as she nudged her. "You also eat slowly, who knows that we'll be able to eat this heavenly food in upcoming few days?" Hayami said. "Tell the others also to eat slowly".

Yuki told everyone. They all started to eat slowly. After twenty minutes, they went to their room. "Okay let us take a thirty-thirty minute sleep!" Hayami said. It was nine-thirty. First Yuki slept. They put a timer of thirty minutes. Till then Hayami packed some juices and snackes, just in case if they wanted to eat something tasty or else they just had to keep themselves energetic by eating a sugary protein-bar. Half and hour passed. "Yuki! Get up dude!", Akari said shaking her. Yuki woke up and went to the washroom. She got freshed and bathed.

Akuma pushed himself on the bed and hugged his pillow. "Turn the AC on!" Akuma said. Hayami glared at him. "Why should I? You were my bodyguard not me!" Hayami said. Akari looked at her in a sceptical manner. "Bodyguard?" Alari asked. "Nothing, just talking about a story I read today", Hayami tried to explain. Akuma giggled. His laugh had a large base as his mouth was covered with the pillow. "You turn it on by your own!", Hayami said as she gazed at him while narrowing her eyes. "Okay dude!" Akuma said as he turned the AC on and slept. "And your thirty minutes start, NOW!" Akari said. *Snore... Snore*

"He slept?!" Hayami looked at him in confusion. "Yes he is asleep", Akari said looking at his eyes. Hayami looked at him in a *nice talent* manner. 15 minutes passesd and it was ten-fifteen. *Click.*

Yuki came out of the washroom. She sat on the chair infront of the mirror and started drying her hairs. "Yuki! You don't need to wear pant-shirt today. Today we'll just walk. Keep it for future because you can't wear frock, who knows if there's rocky way or were mountain type? Go and wear frock", Hayami said in a concertive manner. "Okay", Yuki said as she went in the washroom and changed to a green frock with white firl. 15 minutes passed again. "Akuma! wake up! Go and BATH!" Hayami shouted. Akuma woke up as he scrunched his eyes and streched his body.

"I'm going!" He said as he took the towel and his clothes and went inside. They all slept and then bathed, turn-by-turn. First went, Yuki then Akuma, then Hayami, then Akari. It was ten-forty-five now. Only 15 minutes left for them to fulfill their dream.

XXXI
Chapter 31

"Ready?" Hayami asked as she hung the bag. She was wearing a blue frock with yellow firl and had a bunny hairband on her head, which was of black colour. Akari wore a frock of purple colour. Akuma wore a white T-shirt, with dark blue coloured jacket on it and dark blue coloured cargo. "READY!" Everyone shouted. The home was full of silence. Hinata, Aiko, Hiroshi, Sayuri, all were asleep. Hayami slowly opened the room's door. They creeped outside and walked out. "Wait!" Hayami said. She went to hr parents room, where they both were all asleep. She kissed their heads. She looked around, as she saw a photo frame of their family. She took it out and hugged it tightly. Her eyes were full of tears. "Love you mom! Love you dad!" Hayami whispered. She went to Aiko's and Hinata's room. She gave them a slight hug and pecked them. "I'll miss you all, I don't know whether I'll be able to see you again", she said. She saw a camera kept beside Hinata's bed. On the nightstand. She took it. She saw there were two reels of the same video. She took one and kept in her bag. "Bye!" She looked at them and went to the living room where all her friends assembled. "Let's go guys", she said. They opened the door and came out. Hayami slowly closed the door, not knowing whether she'll come here again or not. She looked at her home, with hopeful and teary eyes at the last time, before going. Off went the door and she closed it as she scrunched her eyes stopping her tears to fall. Yuki hugged her. "I know it's hard", she said. They all started walking. Half an hour passed...

"Have we reached?" Yuki said tiredly. "No, it's two miles more", Hayami said as she looked at the Philia's map. "TWO MILES! ARE YOU SERIOUS!? FOR SURE!" Akari yelled as she gaped and sat down on the road. Hayami sat down to. Everybody settled down. "Let's take a break for two minutes", Akuma said. Suddenly Muriel, Hayami's pet came flying by. "Muriel!" Hayami cried. As he landed down, Hayami saw a box in his hand. "What's this?" Hayami said as she carefully took that box out of his talons. She opened it. "What's in there?" Yuki asked impatiently. "It is-"...

XXXII
Chapter 32

"Strawberries?" Hayami said looking at the pile of strawberries scattereed her and there in the box. "Why do we need that?" Akari said. "Wait guys, strawberries, i-it means that, umm- WE CAN EAT THEM BECOME A DRAGON AND THEN FLY TILL THERE!" Hayami said. "Yeah nice idea, our legs won't hurt either. But maybe our hands would", Akuma said. "Dragon?" Yuki said. "I mean we are actually going to try becoming a dragon?"

"Yay! I'm so excited! As well as scared", Akari said as she jumped. "YOur legs aren't hurting now?" Hayami said. Akari looked down and then took one strawberry from that box. "Take two three at a time", Hayami instructed. She again put her hand in the box and took two to three pieces. They all took one by one.

BOOM! They all became dragons. "Wow!!!" Yuki and Akari said as they looked at their scales which were shimmering in the bright moonlight. "They arepretty right?" Akuma said flexing his claws. "Mine are the best!" When they all looked at their scales, they started to look at each others. "WOW! HAYAMI'S ARE THE BEST ONE!" Yuki said in a slow motion. They all turned their eyes at Hayami's. "Bro! I want to have those. They're so shiney!", Akuma said as he looked at her wings. "They look so cool!" Akari said grazing her hands on her head. "Now don't look at yourselves, LET'S FLY!" Hayami said as she flapped her wings. "Okay!" Yuki, Akari and Akuma said as they strenched their talons and then flew away. "It feels so good while flying!" Yuki said, feeling the breeze. "My body feels so light!" Akari said. They all flew and flew. Finally one hour passed. They all saw a mountain. The atmosphere there was were foggy and misty. "I can see something between the moutains", Hayami said as she narrowed her eyes because of air pressure. "THE MOUNTAIN HOLE!" Akari said as she crashed onto Hayami as she lost her balance. "Ow!" Hayami cried. "You should learn balancing your wings", Hayami said. Finally the reached. They softly landed on the mountain's legs. "Wow! The mounutain hole is actually very small", Hayami said remembering what Hinata and Aiko had told her regarding it. "Let's start digging it", Yuki said. They all sprinkled few drops of water, which they got from a nearby pond. Slowly-slowly, they became back to normal. "Akuma, bring the shovels for all of us", Hayami said. Akuma went, opened his bag and took out four shovels from his bag. "Here you all go", he said and they all started digging it. Many hours passed. It was 4:00 AM in the morning. They all took a break then digged, took a break and then digged more. "It's too exhausting", Yuki said as she wiped her sweat. "It's almost done, Akuma! Try getting your head out of it", Hayami said as she threw her shovel down. Akuma drank some water and then went towards the hole. He slowly tried to fit his head, as he held the ferns and roots aside. He was successful. "Yay!!! Finally!" They all cheered together. "First Hayami will step out", Akuma said. "Yes, as it was all Hayami's idea, she'll got first", Akari said. "Go Hayami! Fullfill your dream", Yuki said. Hayami sighed and then took a step forward. Getting thousands of butterflies in her stomach she finally stepped out. "Congratulations!" They all said. Hayami smiled as her eyes were full of tears.

XXXIII

Chapter 33

They all- not inside, but

WENT OUTSIDE. "Wow! It looks so heavenly", Yuki said. "It feels like I'm breathing oxygen for the first time", Akari said. "I've been a lot many times out and in though nut, yeah, when it was my first time, I also felt this much good only", Akuma said. "Let's start walking!" Hayami said. "Let's go!" They all said.

Stamp slither... Stamp slither...

"Umm Guys? Did you hear anything?" Hayami said as she scrunched her eyebrows. "Ya, I think so a voice came from there", Akari said. Suddenly a man popped behind from them. "Ahhh", they all yelled but a little slowly. "Who are you all! INTRUDERS!" The man said softly. Akuma looked at him in confusion. "Why aren't you shouting at us if you think we are intruders?" Akuma asked suspiciously. The man gulped. "Hide behind the bushes! There's a bear roaming out there".

"Bear? What's that?" Yuki asked. "You don't know about them? Okay fine- just know that they can kill you in just one push!" That man said as he ran away. "Let's go and hide!" Akari said. They all went and sat behind the bushes. They slowly peeped out. They could hear some weird noices. *Stamp Slllitherrr....*

They all gulped except, Akuma. He was a gutsy boy. "Please ss-top it, I-I am n-new here!" Hayami said nervously as she was at the last. Akuma was sitting in the first row, second were Akari and Yuki and last Hayami sat there. "Don't worry Hayami, it's just a bear", Akuma said. Akari was hugging Yuki tightly. "I said I-I am new! We all are new! Please don't kill us!" Hayami's voice rised and now it was ful of terror. "Whom are you talkin-" Akuma said as he was turning back but was then very astonished to even complete his sentence. There were four guards pointing their spear at Hayami. Akari and Yuki fell behind out of fear and horror. "Step back you all!" Akuma shouted at them. "First you all invade in our territory, and then shout at us only!? Silly Brats!" The guards said. The first guard pointed his spear at Hayami tightly. "LEAVE HER!" Akuma shouted. Yuki and Akari were in to much panic to say anything. "First tell us, what's your motive?" The second guard with very big nose asked. "We don't have any motive we just want to go to the Nightpowers community", Yuki said. "AT LEAST NOW LEAVE HER!" Akuma yelled. Hayami's face went purple put of fear. "Shut up! This boy is yelling at us LIKE NOTHING! Who do you think you are huh?" The third guard said which had too much big eyes. Akuma then took out a paper from his pocket and then slapped it on the first guard's face. As soon as that guard opened it, Akuma said, "Queen Yasha's, the Queen of the Nightpowers's certified ASSASSIN!"

The guards gulped. They kept their spears down and then bowed in front of him. Akuma smirked. Suddenly, ROAR!!!

A bear collapsed onto the fourth guard and tore his hat apart. "Run guys!" Akari shouted. They started running. "The closest place where we think we can be safe is-is the Mountain hole. Let's try to go there!" Hayami said. They all ran as fast as they could. The so-very hungry bear followed them till the end. "Where is the whole!" Yuki yelled in terror. "It has disappered!" Akari shouted. Hayami stared at the mountain, where there was a big hole digged by them and now, disappered. "What we'll do now?" Akuma said. Hayami looked at it. How will they survive now- outside their Diamond community, which was a totally new place for them, and from the people, who were around to kill them?

THE ADVENTURE CONTINUES IN
TALONS OF POWER
BOOK TWO: MEETING THEIR LOST HEIRS
----------*WILL BE PUBLISHED IN NEXT YEAR*--------